SECRETS IN THE FOREST

TINA POTTER

KENNY DIETRICH

Cover and art b

I

DEDICATIONS

From Tina

For my husband Ryan: my greatest adventure
began when I married you. You're a huge
blessing to my life, thank you for being mine.

From Kenny

In honor of my friend Jeff, and in loving
memory of my Mother

Preface

Thank you for picking up the first book of the Survival Ember series. Inside this book you'll find elements of intrigue, a strong sense of faith, and the strength of the family unit all lined with the powerful mindset of survivalism.

The story is told from two different point of views: Ember and her father, John. Written by Tina, Ember's point of view is that of a young, spunky 16 year old girl who ends up stumbling across something dark in those woods. John, her father and written by Kenny, is raising Ember as a strong capable girl and works as a trapper and local handyman.

As you read this survival based fiction, the authors hope you enjoy the book but more importantly that you may learn a thing or two.

CHAPTERS

IV

"survivalism noun
sur·viv·al·ism | \ sər-ˈvī-və-ˌli-zəm \
Definition of survivalism:
an attitude, policy, or practice based on the
primacy of survival as a value"

Survivalism. (n.d.) In Merriam-Webster's
dictionary. Retrieved from https://
www.merriam-webster.com/dictionary/
survivalism

BOOK ONE

CHAPTER ONE

Ember

I watched my dad, John, demonstrate the art of fire building. The sun shone high at late afternoon, and a breeze was beginning to flow through the camp. As Dad spoke to our survival class, I tuned out for a moment and listened to the berating sounds of a woodpecker echoing through the hills of the forest.

As I looked around, my senses came alive with all that I loved so much: the earthy aroma of the pines and the forest floor, the birdcalls breaking into the stillness, and the sight of all the backpacks and rucksacks hanging lazily from the nearby trees. Everyone had picked what they thought would be a good spot for the night and claimed it as their own personal campsite. Now Dad would start with a lesson on fire, and then teach how to build a shelter with the small tarps that the students had brought.

Their packs were light, but everyone had the necessary gear to survive the night. Each student had had to pack the required list of items, but they could bring whatever else they thought they might need to smooth the roughness of the trip. Dad had warned of overpacking, and most people heeded this warning, but there was always one who found a way to pack more than they needed. Dad's "minimal" list included a five-by-seven-foot lightweight backpacking tarp, a sleeping bag or blanket (appropriate for the weather), a fixed-blade knife, a ferro rod for starting fires, a metal water container or canteen, a mess kit, a small first aid and hygiene kit, a hundred feet of paracord, a small flashlight or headlamp, a change of socks, and a small amount of food sealed in an airtight bag.

My dad's voice caught my attention, and I snapped out of my daydream. "Building a fire is all about preparation. Abraham Lincoln was quoted as saying, 'Give me six hours to chop down a tree, and

I will spend the first four hours sharpening the axe'."

Dad had created four different piles of dried material, sticks, and wood. He raised a softball-sized birds' nest of dried grass and the bark of a dead tree in his hand and explained, "This absolutely has to stay dry. I have kept this in my pocket since I gathered it, and I didn't bring it out until I was ready to use it." He pointed to the next pile of small pencil-sized sticks and went on, "I'm not as worried about the rest of these. I don't want them to be wet, but a little bit of moisture won't hurt them. Now, let's place the birds' nest on the raft we prepared."

He placed the tinder on the pieces of wood he had laid down beforehand, and then he reached for the ferro rod on his belt. In the wilderness, Dad always wore a fixed-blade knife with a thick blade, a ferrocerium rod (or a "ferro rod") used to create high-temperature sparks, a dump pouch that rolled up when not in use, and a folding handsaw with an eight-inch blade.

The ferro rod was secured to his leather knife sheath through a loop made especially for the tool. The ferro rod also had a paracord lanyard that attached it to a loop with a snap that went around his belt vertically so he would not lose it. A ferro rod is an essential piece of equipment for starting fires.

I watched as people lined up to try it themselves. One by one, they each struggled, just as I still do occasionally, to get that one spark that would set the nest ablaze. The day had been warm—the evidence of that was found in the sweat on our brows—but it was cooling down quickly, and come night we would be thankful for our efforts of building a fire. We needed food, too, and while Dad had some of his freeze-dried survival food pouches in his rucksack, this time he suggested that it be my job to help the group learn how to identify and gather wild edibles—a sort of test of my own knowledge.

See, Dad had learned quite a bit about identifying wild edibles on his own, but his strengths and interests had always been more focused on other areas of survival, such as gear, shelter building, search and rescue, etc. I would listen to Dad as he tried to teach me all he knew about survival, and even though I've learned so much from him, my curiosity in plants grows even stronger to this day.

I found it particularly interesting that throughout history, people have used plants for everything from food to clothing, shelter, and medicine. In the Bible, God speaks of plants for many uses. Some plants were recognized for their purifying properties, such as hyssop in Psalm 51:7, or myrrh and other unspecified herbs in Esther 2:12. Some plants could be used as materials in crafting, such as the bulrushes Moses' mother made into an ark in Exodus 2:3. For clothing, linen is spoken of in Exodus 35:25; it is derived of plant material. I liked looking at the research being done on biblical plants these days, and I found it interesting that some of the plants that were used for purification in biblical times have been proven today as antibacterial or antimicrobial.

"Ember?" A voice called me back to reality.

"Sorry, just thinking."

One of Dad's eyebrow shot up, and he looked at me quizzically.

"Care to share?"

"Just thinking about plants. We gotta eat next, right?" Some of the people in the crowd chuckled, while others nodded vigorously. It was clear we were all ready to restore some of the calories we had burned on the hike.

"I was getting to that, actually. I don't know about you guys, but food is one of the closest things to a man's heart, in my opinion. Thankfully, my daughter specializes in sharing this part of the class."

I was nervous at that. No matter how many times I spoke in front of a crowd, wrenching gut pains always made an appearance. It was time to grit my teeth and just do it—and do it well! I couldn't let Dad down.

"I wouldn't call myself an expert or anything like that, but I do know a thing or two. If anyone is interested in gathering some food, follow me..."

One of the many reasons Dad and I had specifically chosen this area for our class was the flora growing around. It being early autumn, there were still some relatively simple plants to identify. It would get harder the later it got in the year, as the flowers would die off and the nutrients returned to the roots of the plants. I wasn't that great at identifying plants simply by their roots and remains.

As we walked, I decided to share some tips. "It's a good idea to plan as you go, whether you're backpacking for fun or you're in a survival situation. For me, I like to gather as I see the plants so that I will have food when the time comes. This may seem unnecessary, but it's rather important because you may see some plants you can use for food when you're not hungry, but later when the time comes, you may be racked with hunger and those plants may not be around the area you find yourself in. It may be dark, it could be storming, or you could find yourself stuck somewhere, and you might have to sit tight and go without. There are many things a person can do without in this world, but food is not one of them, in my opinion."

"That's for sure," said Dad. "And constant refueling of calories lost is vital. You might not be able to take in as much as you lose, but you do need to try. Calories equal energy, and in situations where you could find yourself fighting for your life, energy is everything."

I looked back at Dad and smiled. People didn't tend to think like that, but they should. Even I found myself taking for granted the easy access of meals three times a day, guaranteed snacks for when I felt my blood sugar levels start to drop, and the little energy I had to spend getting those meals. I wondered if the people in this course really could understand that. Dad had learned the importance of not taking food for granted; he had learned that lesson all too well when he found himself stuck without food while on a backpacking trip at Yosemite. I remember Dad telling me the story on one of our camping trips about six years ago when I had just turned ten.

"I was eighteen years old and set off on my first backpacking trip. I was three days into backpacking through the Grand Canyon of the Tuolumne, and it had been storming for two of the three. I was continuing my way down along the Tuolumne River, past White Cascade Falls, when I decided to set up camp. The rain had slowed, letting up for what I hoped would be an hour or two, and it looked like the skies were clearing. I suppose I could've have rescheduled this trip, but I had the week scheduled off from school and felt like it was 'now or never.' The weather forecast showed signs of clear skies within four days of having set out, and I knew I could rough it until then. It'd make for the adventure." he stated.

"It made for a good story," I replied, not realizing just how important it was that I listened to him as he told it.

"I set up my shelter, still relatively new at backpacking. I didn't realize that location was key and that where I set up would be almost a fatal mistake. I had figured that sleeping ten feet from the river would be a wise decision. Having set up my ultralight backpacking tent, changed into some dry clothes, and put down my bedroll and mat, I lay there quietly, enjoying that my decisions had led me to that moment in my life. Who wouldn't enjoy falling asleep to the relaxing sound of the river's water? I was on my first backpacking trip and had so much to be grateful for. The moon shone heavy and full that night, and the stars were bright as I thanked God one last time before nodding off...but then the clouds began to roll in and another storm had arrived.

"I woke out of my exhausted slumber with a start to the sound of thunder and the uncomfortable feeling of being sopping wet. Looking back, I realized I had been dreaming that I had fallen asleep in a bathtub while still fully clothed. I woke up to a disappointed surprise: The river had now become roaring loud and water had gotten into my tent. As I opened the flap, I found it wasn't the rain but the river itself that had invaded my privacy. I moved quickly, rebuking myself for having not thought about choosing higher ground or possibly even camping a farther distance away from the river. With the flash flood, the water was now up to a few inches in my tent and I would be in trouble if I didn't act quickly.

"But I couldn't focus on the tent at that moment. I had to worry more about my supplies and keeping them safe and dry. No chance of that, though. I hadn't realized that I had left my backpack open, and when I had opened my tent flap, some of the supplies quickly escaped in the current. I wasn't even sure what I had lost, but I needed to know what I had at the moment. I felt around the water in the tent for what was left and then threw on my backpack, ready to make my escape to higher ground.

"My clothes stuck to me as the rain beat down and the wind whipped viciously about. Lightning struck, and thunder sounded. I called out to God and begged Him to keep me safe. God answered with the slowing of the rain and quieting of the thunder. The storm had passed, and I took shelter in a recess in a rock wall.

"After the rain had ended and the wind had died down, I decided to move forward. Knowing that going back wasn't an option, I climbed to higher ground and found an area where I could once again set up shelter. All that was left in my backpack were a 5x7 tarp, a ruined flashlight, a knife, a ferro rod, a paracord bracelet, and some of my cooking gear. I quickly set to work on building a shelter. After unfolding the paracord bracelet and taking it apart, I tied it between two trees. Next, I set my tarp up on it and stumbled around for heavy rocks to place and anchor the tarp down."

That's when Dad discovered that he didn't need so many supplies when backpacking. That's when he first became a survivalist.

Someone from the group—I think his name was Eric—pointed out a dying plant.

"Isn't this lamb's ear?"

"Well, I can see why you would think that, but it's actually mullein. Even though it has that almost furry resemblance on the leaves, lamb's ear is almost grayish, and mullein is more green. Lamb's ear will stay smaller than mullein, with a stalk of purple flowers growing from the center, while mullein will grow larger, up to ten feet, and it will have a stalk of yellow flowers. Another difference is that mullein leaves will grow with a rosette center and lamb's ear won't."

"It's edible, though, right? I think I remember my grandpa telling me about mullein," said a woman on Eric's right.

"Correct! Mullein is edible, but I prefer it raw than cooked. Some of you might feel the other way around. It's a bit of a bitter herb, so I would incorporate it with another wild edible to take the edge off."

I stepped over and grabbed one of the few remaining good leaves from the plant and started passing it around. Everyone ripped a piece off to taste; some shrugged while others spit it out.

"Not the most pleasant-tasting of plants, I'll agree." I couldn't deny it. "However, what this plant lacks in taste it makes up for in medicinal value. A poultice of this plant can help soothe burns and scrapes, and a tea made from these plant leaves is fantastic for upper respiratory troubles or a nasty cough, and it can take the edge off of a cold. For those wanting to incorporate it into a meal, go ahead and take some. Either way, let's start moving on to the next plant. I think I see wild carrot over here."

After a while spent gathering and discussing herbs, we finally made it back to where we had camped for the night. Someone complained of a blister on their foot, and Dad passed one of my salves over. Laying out the herbs I had gathered, I started preparing dinner. In my pack I had a chicken bouillon cube, a small camp cookpot, and some water I had gathered from a stream earlier that was now in my filtering water bottle. Thankfully, we were near the stream in case more was needed. As I finished laying things out, everyone gathered near.

"Of course, you all will be preparing your own meals tonight as practice, but I wanted you to try a favorite of mine. For a soup made up of roots and leaves you might not find it as appetizing as something you would cook at home, but for food we just grabbed out of the forest, it won't be too bad. There should be enough for you all to have a small cup to try. Then, I would love to come around and see what you guys come up with yourselves! Survival food doesn't have to be boring. It can actually be kind of fun."

"As long as I don't start cramping up and making a mess of my pants, I'll be happy!"

Laughter ensued at Eric's joke, and I couldn't help but chuckle.

"Not gonna lie, Eric, I've been there myself." That was another story for another time, though.

I took out my knife and set right to work. I peeled the roots and sliced them up, wiping them clean with a cloth damp from the water I had. I put them in a little baggie and then got to work on making the contraption to hold my pot over the fire. I decided on using the "cooking crane" method and placed a stick with a fork in it into the ground and placed another stick also in the ground that rested in the crotch of the other stick—one end in the ground and the other up in the air. I then placed the handle of my pot on the stick and over the fire. I removed the lid a little later to find the water ready for the bouillon cube and the herbs. I placed in the pot wild carrot root, mullein stem, plantain leaves, dandelion leaves and root, and chicory flowers. We had also stumbled across some wild rosemary, which I placed into the pot for seasoning. I replaced the lid and let it all cook for about ten minutes.

In the meantime, while the others were getting their own fires and meals ready, I started preparing my shelter. I began by tying a line with my paracord from one tree to another at the spot I chose—carefully, I might add—where the trees were about seven feet apart. I kept the ridge line, as it's called, around thigh-high. I kept this low to the ground to be able to trap heat, thus creating a microclimate that I could control with my fire. I pegged down the width of the tarp a foot or so behind the ridge line and draped the other side over the paracord. It allowed about six inches of the tarp to hang down; this helped to trap the heat and kept the weather off of me. I had cut two lengths of cordage, one for each end, to use as guylines and secured the hanging part of the tarp to the ground. I laid down an armful of pine boughs we had cut earlier to create a barrier between me and the cold earth. It was an extremely low shelter, and I had to crawl and wiggle my way in, but I knew it would keep me warm and snug.

I dug a shallow pit in front of my shelter with a thick stick and piled up the dirt on the opposite side, which allowed me to reflect some of the heat from the fire back to me. In the morning when I broke camp I would kick the dirt back over the hole to reduce the footprint I would leave. A pro at starting fires, I quickly got one going. With the pile of fuel wood gathered, I knew I would be comfortable all night long.

A rich aroma drifted over from the fire; the food was ready.

"Hey, y'all! Anyone ready to try my excuse for a soup? Bring whatever you have to drink it in over."

Everyone gathered with their tins or cups. I used a wooden cup, or kuska, that Dad had hand-carved for me and scooped some out for each person. Some didn't think it was all that bad, others actually liked it, but no one disliked it completely. The heat from the soup warmed me deep into my bones as the air had grown chilly.

I crouched on the ground a little ways from the fire and lay back to look up, staring at the stars. That was something I wanted to look more into, and I contemplated the subject that night. I know nothing of stars, except that over there is the Big Dipper. Or is that the Little Dipper? Where's the other one...?

"Hey, kiddo."

My head turned to see Dad's boots, and when I looked up, I saw him grinning down at me. I patted the ground beside me for him to join me.

"The soup didn't turn out half bad. Might be the best meal you've made out here yet."

"I don't know, Dad. I'm pretty sure that time we fried up some chicken of the woods with that poke and added dittany to it really topped this."

"Mmm...that was good, too. Would be great to do that again. If we can't find chicken of the woods, maybe we could use chanterelles."

"I don't know, maybe. Hey, Dad, is that the Big Dipper or the Little Dipper?"

We grew quiet as Dad looked up and over to the constellations that shown bright above. His gray eyes scanned the sky until they settled on what he was searching for.

"Look over there, what do you see?"

I looked up to where he pointed, and sure enough there it was.

"Oh, I didn't see it hiding over there. So that's the Big Dipper, and that one over there is the Little Dipper."

"Last time I checked."

Having propped myself up on my elbows, I looked around frantically for a moment. Okay, then, where is the... Wait, is that it?

"Dad, is that the North Star?"

"Yeah, good job. I'm guessing we should work on learning our stars then? I don't know them too well myself, but I know some of the basics."

A cool breeze went through the campsite, and I shivered.

"I'm going to turn in early, I think. Are you going to stay up with the group and swap stories?"

"I was thinking about it. We'll see how tired some of them are. I'm kind of beat myself."

I hugged him and kissed his cheek. "Love you, Dad. Sleep well. Good night, everyone! I'm turning in early. See y'all at breakfast!" I waved to everyone as I walked over to my shelter and crawled in.

As I lay there, bundled up, warm and safe, a feeling of contentment and peace filled the camp. An owl spoke out into the midnight air, and the wind made the leaves dance into the night. The forest grew quiet, and so did we... Sleep came slowly and then all at once.

CHAPTER TWO

I slung my backpack over the side of the truck into its bed. It was early, and we had just finished hiking back from the campsite. Dad had the truck running to warm up as we wrapped up, thanking everybody for coming. We all said our good-byes, some hugging each other as well, and everyone thanked Dad and me for our services and the fun time they had. As they all started leaving, I looked up and around at the sky as the sun started cresting the ridges. Bright oranges and pinks colored the sky, welcoming the day and bidding the night farewell. No more stars then, save for in the memories of the night before.

"Let's go, kiddo."

I hopped in beside Dad and reached over to turn up the heat. Looking over, I caught Dad pursing his lips and blowing air from his mouth. I grinned and started blowing as well. It was sort of a game between us, but not really in the sense of the word. It just showed our excitement at the coming of the colder weather. Autumn had always been my favorite season, and Dad loved winter. Mom and Tanner both loved summer; they preferred the warmth. I guess it was my love of layering, and the crisp feeling of the cold on my face.

"I need a shower, but I don't want to blow-dry my hair."

"You're not going to church with wet hair, Ember." Dad chuckled at the thought.

I sighed. "I guess not... I could just use dry shampoo."

"As long as you shower, I'm sure you can figure something else out for your hair. Your mom might not agree, though. See what she says and do that."

"Yes, sir."

The truck bounced along the dirt road, and I saw that we weren't far from home. I pressed my cheek against the window, felt the coldness on my cheek and the warmth everywhere else from the heat that came from the vents. Then suddenly we hit a pothole, and my face smacked against the window.

"Ow!"

Dad started laughing, and he smacked the steering wheel while I sat up. Rubbing my cheek, I felt silly and sore.

"That'll probably bruise."

"Just add it to the collection you've got going, Ember."

We arrived at our cozy little home. Smoke that came from the stovepipe peeping out of the roof was a good sign that it was indeed cozy inside. Thanks, Mom! We grabbed our gear and made for what was the garage first. It had been turned into Dad's headquarters for trapping and bushcrafting, kind of like a "man cave," but there was a shelf for me. We walked in and put down our bags. I emptied mine and went through it, placing each item on its designated hook or in its specific box. I knew that it was important to always be organized. I grabbed my dirty clothes from the bag and set them beside Dad's. Lastly, I set my bag directly on my shelf. I would repack it when I got home from church; it's also important to always be ready.

Each family member had their own backpack, packed specifically for them with survival tools to get them through most any night in the woods. Although Mom and Tanner weren't as outdoorsy as Dad and I were, they recognized that preparedness was an important mindset to have and they were ready for whatever might come. We also had a buddy system in place in case the family got separated—I would help Mom and Dad would help Tanner. This was mostly because Tanner was autistic, and Mom wasn't as well-versed in survival techniques as Dad and I were.

I left the garage with the laundry and headed for the house. It was a small place and really old. Upstairs was the kitchen, living room, my parents' room, and the bathroom. Tanner and I each had rooms in the basement.

As I entered the house through the living room and took off my boots, the heat of the wood stove warmed my face. A sweet aroma greeted me as well, and I headed into the kitchen.

"Hey, Mom! Is that apple crumble I smell?"

"Welcome home! I missed you guys. It is apple crumble, and it's ready to eat. Go take a shower, and I'll have a plate made up for you."

I kissed her cheek, dropped my boots by the back door, and headed for my room in the basement.

It was a small basement. Once you reached the bottom of the basement stairs, directly in front of you was a deep freeze filled with game that Dad had hunted and vegetables that Mom had grown. To your left you'd see a door, and to your right you'd see a curtain. The door led to Tanner's room; the curtain to mine. Mine had a curtain because I had accidentally kicked a hole in the door while practicing my self-defense. I guess you could say the doors were pretty thin—I think they were made of some kind of plywood or something—but Dad was gonna fix it anyways.

I entered my room and reached for the string to turn the light on. On one side of the room was my bed, on the other was a dresser and vanity. Photos and trophies were on top of my dresser, and my recurve bow hung above it. There was also a quiver of arrows beside the dresser, along with a stack of books. Random sketches I'd made of plants and animals I'd seen on my hikes were taped on the walls.

After snagging a fresh change of clothes from the drawers of the dresser, I turned to leave. In my rush, I almost plowed right into my brother.

"H-hey, sis. W-what are you up to?"

"Sorry, I was rushing off to take a shower. Did you sleep well last night?"

Tanner shrugged.

"I slept fine, I guess. D-did you enjoy camping?"

"Yeah, it was nice. I'll tell you all about it at breakfast."

"Cool."

Like I said earlier, Tanner is autistic, and although it was hard for him at times, he tried to be as independent as possible in spite of it. Autism showed itself in Tanner in ways of his speech (the stammering) and in the little tics in his behavior. I was proud of his daily fight to overcome it.

I walked into the bathroom and proceeded to clean away the residue of the past day. After stepping into the shower, I turned on the water and let it run down my face, feeling renewed.

Mom had already set the table, and Tanner and Dad were ready. When I got back to the kitchen and took a seat, I bowed my head as Dad led us in prayer.

"Father, thank You for Your blessings and mercy. Thank You for bringing Ember and me back safe and for watching over Maria and Tanner while we were gone. Continue watching over us, Lord, and bless the hands that prepared this meal. In Your wonderful name we pray, amen."

"I want to hear about the trip," Mom said. "Your dad says you did well."

"Yeah, I was nervous. It was my first time preparing the meal for the others. I figured most of them wouldn't like it, but I guess they did."

"I thought it was good," said Dad. "You know what I do like, though? Seeing people developing or sharing the same passion we have."

"Yeah, it's kind of cool to see people start wanting to live more conscious of what's around them..."

"And to start thinking about being prepared if something were to go wrong in today's unstable environment."

We finished breakfast, and I asked if I could ride with Tanner to church. The subject of the survival course would soon become a fond memory and a learning experience about Dad's passion in life. Everyone left the table to help Mom by taking our dishes to the sink and cleaning up before continuing to get ready for church.

Tanner and I drove the truck to church while Dad and Mom took the car. Tanner loved driving, a sign of his own kind of determination for self-reliance.

When we arrived at church, it was already full. It was a small church, recently built, but the congregation wasn't new at all. Rocky Falls Church used to meet across town in the old church building, but the structure had grown decrepit and was falling apart. After much discussion, the congregation agreed on building a new one elsewhere. They found land for sale at a cheap price and liked the location. They purchased it and soon were building what we now had as the church building and fellowship hall.

Kids ran through the parking lot, and parents called out to each other. Old Man Collier and his family had just pulled in, and Dad walked over to chat with them about the events of the weekend. Mom, Tanner, and I went inside to find our seats.

"Mom, Chelsea's already here. Can I go talk to her?"

"That's fine, but come sit with us when you hear the piano."

I headed over to chat with my best friend, Chelsea Powell. She had curly, raven-black hair with frosty blue eyes and had a temper at times. She was sitting with her little sister, Annalee, and was trying to get the girl to stay seated. Clearly, Annalee shared her sister's feistiness.

"Hey, Chels, how's your weekend going?"

Chelsea let out a huff.

"Good, but Annalee is driving me nuts. She's not been listening to Mom or me at all this weekend."

Annalee, only two years old, stood up on the pew and stuck out her tongue at Chelsea. Chelsea and I just rolled our eyes.

"Anyway, how was the camping trip, Ember?"

"I'd like to refer to it as 'backpacking,' but it went pretty great. I got the chance to speak about herbs..."

My eyes had been scanning the crowded pews, and my voice trailed off when I noticed a cute boy about my age take a seat next to an older woman toward the back of the church.

"Who is that?"

Chelsea turned around and searched the crowd.

"Who?"

"That guy with Mamaw Dawson. Who is he?"

"Oh, I had heard that Mamaw Dawson's grandson was coming to live with her for a while. From what I know, after his mom died he hasn't gotten along well with his dad, so he decided to move out here with his grandma. He's from the city, you know."

Of course, Chelsea knew the scoop on him. She kept her ears to the ground for everything happening in Rocky Falls. Our talk was cut short, though, as the pianist started the call to worship. I headed back to the pew where my family was seated and took my place beside them. Mom had quietly opened a small roll of candy and slipped a piece in my hand. As the preacher began to direct the service with a deep, bellowing voice, the sweet bite of mint softened onto my tongue. I turned my head, watching Annalee squirm in her seat beside Chelsea, then turned to look at the new guy. As soon as his eyes met mine, I turned back toward the front and felt my face flush with the heat of my embarrassment. Suddenly, I noticed that Dad was looking at me. He gestured toward the pulpit. Eyes up front, young lady.

Right—sorry, Dad.

CHAPTER THREE

John

After I dropped Ember off at school, I guided my old pickup truck, the one I affectionately called "Nelly," to Old Man Collier's farm. The truck practically knew the way herself, but every once in a while I would have to give her a nudge right or left. She was kind of like an old mule that Papaw had named Harold that would go straight as an arrow until you yelled "gee" or "haw."

I drove up the gravel road until it became two dirt tracks. The land belonged to the Colliers and was on the back side of a well-maintained farm consisting of approximately seven hundred acres. Man, did they know how to keep a place! It was squared away, as we used to say in the military. This part of their land was mainly used by the family for hunting, and it ended where the federal land began. The adjacent federal land was a forest consisting of three thousand acres, and together it gave me access to a total of almost four thousand acres, once you included my meager parcel of land.

I had been buying up the land around me piece by piece until I reached the Colliers' place. I had recently reached an agreement, or a barter if you will, with Old Man Collier himself to allow me to use his farm and land for the outdoor classes I taught. Since I worked part-time as a nuisance trapper, I had agreed to clean out the coyotes that had invaded his acreage and had been threatening his livestock. I'd continue to keep it free of predators and nuisances in return for the access. The Colliers were good people—I knew they were good for their word.

I drove up the tracks until they disappeared into what became the fringe of the forest. The undergrowth appeared to be massive and dense with briars and brambles. But once I got about fifteen yards in and past all the mess, it opened up into an old-growth forest. The forest floor was clear of undergrowth and beautifully carpeted with leaves and moss. It was like stepping back in time, to a land untouched by humans. I'm sure there were a lot of

49

loggers who would have loved to get their hands (and their saws) on those enormous trees, but the owners wouldn't have it that way, thank goodness.

Grabbing the gearshift on the column, I placed the truck in Park, turned the key in the ignition to shut off the engine, and swung open my door. As I exited into the tall grass, I reached across the bench seat to grab my backpack and then slid my arms through the straps. When I was buckled up, I removed my rifle from the mount secured to the middle of the console and closed the door, ready to be on my way. Soon I was past the brush and into the breathtaking forest.

I pulled my compass out from a pouch on my belt and shot a bearing to get an idea of the direction I was heading. I found a good point to focus on as I walked and took in the fresh autumn air. I'd been there before once, with Mr. Collier. He liked to talk a lot—and slowly, so I was trying to concentrate on the conversation instead of the terrain. That's how most people get lost, not paying attention while they hike.

After serving on the search and rescue team for a few years by that point, I'd rescued many people who told me that very thing. "I just wasn't paying attention," they would say. Another problem is that people spot an amazing view or a spectacular place on social media and think they need to go. With the information at their fingertips, they know where it is and how to get there, but they don't understand everything else involved in the journey. Most rescue victims become victims because they don't prepare. By that, I mean people need to look at the weather, the miles to be hiked, how the terrain is rated, the elevation gains, and even the descents.

After ascending a steep hillside, I found myself at my first destination, an old oak tree that had fallen over, exposing a massive root ball. The roots ran out from the bottom like the snakes on Medusa's head. I stopped and took it in for a moment, and then looked around at the rest of my surroundings. This was the perfect place to set my first coyote snare. The downed tree helped form one side of the funnel I was going to create to steer them into my trap. I started placing brush and debris a lot like a fence, shaping a narrow path of least resistance, right into my snare. Animals are like humans in this aspect; they usually take the easiest paths, too.

I recognized the tracks and game trails of the coyotes all around this area, which was not too far from the farm. The ridge I was on made a gentle curve, like a crescent, and continued deeper into the forest. This was part of a trail system I'd been working on for years, and it would later become part of the trail. I planned on connecting it to what I affectionately called the "Appalachian Interstate."

The Appalachian Interstate is a series of ridges, hills, and cliffsides connected by vines, ropes, ladders, and ziplines. I'd kept it quiet, and no one else knew about it except my confidante, Ember. Maria said it was too dangerous for our little girl to be out in the woods swinging from tree to tree like a monkey, but if my wife could only see the ways Ember handled herself, not to mention the smile it put on her face. Oh, sure, there were a few ladders that could use some repair, but if it held me, it'd hold Ember for sure.

After setting the first snare, I moved on to the next one. Like so many other things in life, trapping is a numbers game. You can't set too many if you want to catch something. I was using the good snares I'd just picked up at the flea market the other day. Normally I used my homemade penny snares, but sometimes they'd fail and the animal would escape. However, these traps were very important, and it was imperative that I get it right. The quicker I removed these darned coyotes from his land, the quicker Mr. Collier would be happy.

I continued setting traps as I walked the ridgeline, looking right and left over each side of the steep hillsides. The ridge was narrow, about as wide as my truck was long. I could see how a predator would love this vantage point...being able to survey the hunting ground and look down on his prey. It was no wonder the coyotes frequented this spot.

Then something caught my eye. My first reaction was to hit the deck, as they say. I immediately dropped flat and lay motionless for the first thirty seconds, trying to figure out what I had just seen. Then it hit me—I wasn't in the sandy battlefields of Iraq. What I saw wasn't an enemy patrol, but just a group of hikers. As I began to control my breathing, I thought to myself how unusual it was to see anyone out there.

I lay prone for a few beats longer and listened to the sounds of the forest. The light breeze blew, the birds were still chirping...but there were no sounds of people. I slowly raised my head to appraise my situation, and to my surprise I saw the hikers right below me. My heart started racing again. Man, they were moving quietly —it was eerily quiet. It was a group of young women, possibly girls Ember's age, led by a female a little older than the rest, and dressed a lot better. She looked like she belonged out there; the other girls looked misplaced wearing rags, old backpacks, and tattered shoes. The other thing that stood out about the leader was her hair: a well-maintained blond ponytail.

I felt obligated to say something to them. Mr. Collier wouldn't take too kindly to people trespassing on his land. I slowly got to my feet and quietly started to descend the hillside. I went unnoticed until I was about ten yards away from the leader, when she must have caught me in her peripheral vision and she suddenly spun around. I held up my empty hands with my palms facing her.

"Whoa, ladies, I mean no harm. I didn't intend to startle you."

I noticed the leader's hand down by her side and slightly behind her back. I couldn't really tell what she was doing, but my instincts told me she had her hand on a pistol...or at the very least, a knife. Finally she brought her empty hand around to the front of her body and slowly smiled, showing perfect white teeth.

"Why, I am so sorry, mister. We were just passing through, and we didn't mean to do anything wrong," she said as she batted her eyelashes.

"Passing through from where...to where? There is nothing even close for miles," I said with an unintentional sound of irritation.

"I'm new to this area and was leading our group through the forest. We must have gotten off the trail. Isn't this part of the federal park?" she asked with a soft voice.

I calmed down a bit and thought about the situation. There were three things that jumped out at me here. One: I didn't know for sure if she had anything behind her back. Two: She just might be telling the truth. And three: The Bible said in Hebrews, "Do not neglect to show hospitality to strangers, for thereby some have entertained angels unawares."

"Well, you're not too far off. However, this is private land, and as a caretaker I can speak for the owners and say he wouldn't like you all wandering around out here. If you keep going on this path, in about ten minutes you'll see another path that veers to the left. Take that path and you'll end up back in the right forest. Otherwise you'll end up in the river, and I'm sure you don't want that."

Her smile widened a little more, showing me more of her pearly whites. "You're right, we wouldn't want that, thank you so much. I'm so sorry to have bothered you. We'll be on our way and out of your hair." She turned to the other girls, who all had their heads down, and gave what reminded me of marching orders. "Okay, girls, you heard the man. Let's get moving."

I squinted my eyes, deep in thought, and when the gears in my brain started turning again, I noticed a far different demeanor than what she had just used with me. I thought to myself, Where is her map and compass, or GPS, or phone even? As if she could read my thoughts, she looked back at me over her shoulder, and I quickly snapped out of it.

As I pretended to be arranging my gear, I watched them trudge off. One of the girls in the middle of the group, the one wearing a red and white flowered scarf, looked like she was ill. Her hair was thin, her cheeks were sunken in, and there were noticeable dark circles under her eyes. Maybe I was overreacting; maybe she was just tired. The whole thing was very strange, and I couldn't help feeling that something just wasn't right.

I started back up the hill from where I had come, and I realized I hadn't made arrangements to quickly climb this part of the trail yet. I didn't have any ladders, ropes, or vines in place to assist me. I made a mental note to bring some along on my next trip. I finally made it the top of the ridge and worked diligently to finish setting the coyote traps.

As I worked, I couldn't help but continually replay the events that had just transpired. I thought about the girls, the brief conversation, the entire exchange, and tried to make sense of it all. Eventually I found myself back at my truck, wondering how I'd gotten there. I was so deep in thought I must have been on autopilot.

Chapter Four

Even after putting in three or four days of hard labor, I couldn't stop thinking about the morning when I'd run into the lady in the woods. I was replacing some drywall and making some other repairs for a lady in our church. My main source of income was handyman work. Nowadays I guess it would be considered "handyperson" work, to be politically correct. Regardless, it was always an honest day's work for an honest day's pay. Maria said I should charge more for my services, but I felt like I had reasonable rates. Plus, I got a lot of referrals and sometimes a pie or baked goods out of it.

I wrapped up the job and cleaned up my mess, although there was usually not much to do afterward since I cleaned as I went. Then I packed everything up in my truck. I was still deep in thought as I started to back out of the woman's driveway, when out of nowhere a black late-model SUV came barreling down the small street. I pressed my foot on the brake, and Nelly stopped abruptly rocking back and forth with the old shocks, missing the passing vehicle within inches. The driver of a really nice Range Rover had just sped by without a care, or even a pause. Then it hit me...and I couldn't believe it... It was the woman in the woods!

Dumbfounded, I sat in the truck and stared out the window down the street at the back of the vehicle in the distance. I realized Mrs. Jackson was looking at me through the glass in her front storm door; she must have heard the tires screech. I waved, gave her a smile, and mouthed, "I'm okay." After looking both ways, again, I released the brake and began driving again down the street.

I thought she was supposed to be backpacking with the girls in the forest. Or did she ever actually say that's what she was doing? I thought about following her and even gave the old truck some gas, but the woman was long gone, nowhere in sight. At the stop sign at the end of the street, I took a minute to collect my thoughts. A car coming up behind me helped me make the decision to move on to my original destination.

When I pulled up to Ember's school, she was already waiting outside. She was beautiful like her mother, and her hair shone like a chestnut in the late afternoon sun. She greeted me with a smile that always warmed my heart, a smile only a daughter could give to her father. I knew I was truly blessed to have such a wonderful family.

"Hey, kiddo!" I said loudly over the noise of the truck's engine.

"Hey, Pops, how was your day?"

I opened with, "Let me tell you about my day," and I recounted the day's events, not skipping any details, right down to the red flowered scarf. She listened patiently. Ember has always been a good listener, and when I was done she sat quietly looking out the passenger-side window as we drove along the country road. I could tell she was processing it all, and I gave her all the space she needed to come to her conclusions. I valued her opinion, as she was wise beyond her years.

The silence was broken when she reached for her go-bag and started to remove her gear. It was the bag she kept ready on her shelf in the garage, or the "man cave," as she affectionately called it. I had grabbed her bag on my way out that morning, knowing she'd want to go to the woods after school to unwind. If there was ever a doubt whether she wanted to go or not, I knew that day's events would remove such a doubt. My girl loved an adventure.

"Let's go check the traps," she said while shedding her good coat and replacing it with her favorite field jacket, which I kept in the truck. Actually, her mom made me keep her field jacket in my truck because she said it stunk and "smelled like a boy." Whatever that was supposed to mean! Ember is a bit of a tomboy, and hygiene wasn't always at the forefront of her attention. Tanner was just the opposite—he always smelled like soap and was extremely clean.

I could tell the wheels in her mind were still turning while she changed her shoes and laced up her boots. "Okay, I can't take it any longer. What do you think, kiddo?"

"Huh? Oh, yeah. I was just thinking about the girls you described. Nothing sounds familiar about them, and I would know of any outdoor activities revolving around girls my age. And wouldn't that woman still be out there with them if she was a guide? There aren't any other guide services in town except ours."

She ran the leather belt I had made for her through the loops on her jeans, then attached a small pouch and her fixed-blade knife to her right side. Snapping on a paracord bracelet, she continued to reach into the backpack for more equipment.

"I just think it's odd…"

We hit a bump in the road as we got closer to the Collier farm, and the road grew increasingly less favorable for Nelly's shocks. Ember braced herself against being tossed around, and once the road smoothed out again, I caught her rubbing her still-sore cheek.

"I just think it's odd that she said they were lost way out in that neck of the woods, and then she showed up in town? If she was driving as fast as you say she was, then it sounds like she's familiar with the street, or at least that part of the town."

There was something I hadn't thought of, and that was one of the many reasons I loved talking things out with Ember. She sat quietly until we arrived at the Collier farm. As we drove past, we waved to Mr. and Mrs. Collier, who were sitting on the front porch, and then we headed up to the wilderness. A few minutes and a lot of bumps later, we came to the end of the dirt tracks, and Ember was scrambling out of the truck before I could even put it into Park. I didn't say anything; I was just going to let her do her thing. I fell back a few paces and let her take the lead. We were heading in the right direction when she stopped and looked around. She reminded me of an old hound dog I used to have, sniffing the wind looking for a scent.

She looked at me. "Am I heading in the right direction? Does it feel right?"

"Yes, Em, you are going exactly in the right direction." I pointed to the top of the ridge where the fallen oak tree was. "Right up there is where I was laying the snares. Let's go check them out before we do any more investigating. Besides, the more I think about it, the more I wonder if I was just imagining things."

"Dad, I think you're on to something big. This could be as big as the bank robbery you and Mom talk about."

"Now, don't go all Nancy Drew on me," I said with a smirk.

"Nancy who?"

I was showing my age again. "She was a young female detective in books when I was a kid. Never mind. Let's not get ahead of ourselves. One thing—"

"I know, I know. One thing at a time. First things first and all that," she interjected. We both started up the hillside

at the same time, with our first mission in
mind.

CHAPTER FIVE

Ember

Leaves started to cover the ground, and the satisfying crunching sound they gave off followed me as I headed toward the first trap. I had learned at a young age to be careful around traps and snares when your dad is a woodsman by trade.

We split up as the daylight was shortened that time of year and nightfall came quick. I followed Dad's usual route, keeping my eyes peeled for signs of traps that had gone off.

So far, nothing.

A knocking sound caught my attention. Somewhere in the distance to my right was a woodpecker busy at work. I shaded my eyes from the evening sun coming through the trees and looked for the source of the noise. The sound stopped, and I wasn't sure if the woodpecker had quit or if it had flown off...

Then I spotted her.

A tall, slender, muscular woman with a sleek blond ponytail was taking a shovel and placing dirt into a large hole. She labored at her task diligently.

Stopping and dropping down low to the ground, I crouched behind my bag and some brush. What was she burying and why? Also, why was she on Old Man Collier's land? Nothing added up.

Then, as I tried to make my position more comfortable by maneuvering my weight from one leg to the other, I lost traction and started slipping past the brush and down the embankment. Leaves scattered noisily, and I knew she must have heard. Grabbing my bag, I rushed back up the embankment and started running hard back the way I came. Pushing through brush and flying past trees, I knew I had to get back to Dad. Dad! Where's Dad?

POW!

Birds panicked at the sound of the gunshot, and I dropped face-first onto the ground.

Time stopped.

My breathing stopped.

My heart pounded in my ears...thump-thump, thump-thump...

God, please protect me...

Nervous tears started streaking down my face, and my hands clenched the dirt and leaves. I listened for her...

Nothing.

No footsteps, no sounds.

The forest had grown quiet.

I shakily got up and started running again. My legs felt heavy, I was lightheaded. My lungs were burning with the cooling air.

I finally spotted him, and he turned when he heard me.

"Dad!"

"Ember? What's the matter?"

I ran right into him and hugged him, sobbing into his shirt.

"Ember, honey, tell me what's wrong. What happened?"

I took a deep breath and released it slowly, gathering my thoughts and trying to calm my nerves.

That's when I noticed that Dad was holding his gun. When I peeked behind him, I found a coyote, shot dead.

"You were the one to fire the gun?"

He chuckled at that.

78

"Yes! Is that what this is about?"

I shook my head.

"That woman you were talking about...she's out there." I pointed back toward the thick of the trees.

"She was burying something, something large too. I was watching her when I slipped, and I knew she heard me."

Dad closed his eyes and nodded. "Let's go back there and assess the situation," he said.

Leading the way as we ran back to site where the woman was digging, I felt safer having Dad with me.

We slowed our running to a walk as we approached the area, but the woman was gone. No signs of her were left, save what might have been the concealment of the freshly replaced dirt.

"Let's go look. Maybe we can dig up whatever she was burying—"

Dad stopped me suddenly. "No. Let's go back. It's getting late."

He took out his compass and shot a bearing. Looking around, I noticed Dad was right. The sun had already begun setting, and dusk was at hand. The crickets were loud, and the woodpecker was back. Suddenly I felt completely safe again here in the woods.

As we made our way back down the road toward home, I kept wondering what that woman was doing out there.

"Dad?"

Dad looked deep in thought before giving me his attention.

"Yes, Ember?"

"What do you think she was doing?"

"I don't know, Ember, but whatever we think about it, now we need to keep to ourselves."

"Are you not going to tell Mr. Collier?"

Dad took a moment and exhaled loudly.

"I'll know when it comes time to. I might ask him if he is now allowing hikers on the property, but when I first spoke to the woman, she made it seem as if she was on the property by accident."

"Hmm...then why would she be back? That's the question."

"Yup, or one of the questions, anyways."

Later that evening, after dinner, I lay in bed staring up at the ceiling fan as it spun quietly. Thoughts should be more like that —quiet. They did go 'round and 'round in my head, though, especially thoughts of the day and the woman burying something in the forest. There had to be something going on, and it was all too strange. Then my mind started wandering back to that guy I'd seen in church. I should've walked over and said hello. I should've gotten his name from Chelsea at school. Rolling over onto my side, I was startled to hear a knocking on my wall beside the curtain blocking my doorway.

"C'mon in," I called.

Tanner sheepishly stepped in.

"H-hey, sis…"

"What's up?"

"You should stay home sometimes and spend time in these woods. I gotcha something."

Making room on the bed, I sat up so Tanner could sit down beside me. In his hand was an arrowhead.

"What? Where did you find this? This is great!"

I crouched down beside the bed and reached for an old shoebox that was under it.

"It-it was in the creek bed, near the bank next to the fallen oak."

"Thanks so much. That's my...fifteenth arrowhead?"

I paused to count, and the fifteenth it was.

"What were you doing down by the creek? You prefer the yard."

Tanner got up and checked to see if the basement door at the top of the stairs was open. When he saw that it wasn't, he went on.

"Promise not to tell?"

I stood to meet his eye level.

"What is it?"

"Promise!"

"Okay, okay! What is it?"

Tanner lowered his voice. "I want to trap, too."

I burst out in a chuckle. Was that all? What was with the secrecy?

"I'm being serious, Ember. Dad can't know."

"I have so many questions. Like, for one, what are you planning to trap? Why, and with what? You don't think Dad's gonna notice when one of his traps goes missing —"

Tanner interrupted. "I'm not helpless, Ember, I know what I'm doing. But-but you have to keep this a secret."

"Okay, but why?"

Tanner sat on the bed. "Because I lost my j-job yesterday."

That didn't make any sense. A wave of confusion and concern came over me.

Tanner worked at Rick Albanson's brickyard, where he was respected by both his boss and his coworkers.

"I'm so sorry, but that doesn't make sense."

"Well, Rick says it's only temporary. People are starting to get laid off, and he's only k-keeping the people he can't spare. I guess I don't fall into that category. But I don't want to commit myself to another job when he may hire me back on in a month or two."

Or never.

"Are you worried about college?"

"That's what I'm trying to save for, anyways."

"Well, he probably let you go because those other men might have families to provide for."

"Yeah, but for now I want to try my hand at selling pelts. Dad and Mom can't know because I want to see if I can do this on my own. I want to prove to myself and to others that I can."

I could respect that. Tanner had confided in me once, a while ago, that he felt Mom babied him more than she ever did me. I think that was because she saw his struggles with his autism and she wanted to protect him as much as possible. Apparently, Tanner was tired of playing it safe, though. With that, he left my room. I had all but forgotten about the strange woman in the woods. My brother's resolve inspired a new thought, however—a thought that could turn into a plan.

If he was determined to be self-reliant, so was I.

CHAPTER SIX

John

The next morning, I lay awake in bed staring at the ceiling, thinking about what Ember and I had seen the day before. It was hard to believe that it was just a series of coincidences. I soon realized I might as well kick the covers off and get the day started. No more sleep was coming. I swung my feet around the side of the bed trying not to wake Maria. She was a light sleeper, and with a sigh she rolled over in frustration. Oh well, I'd tried.

After a shower and my first cup of coffee, I started to feel human again, and my head cleared, allowing me to focus. I made a mental list of all the things I needed to do that day, then put the lid on my coffee cup and headed to the "man cave" to grab the things I'd need. My tools for work were already in the truck, so all I really needed was my trapping gear. But today I was planning on trapping something a little bigger...a human being.

Well, okay, I wasn't going to actually trap her. I grabbed a trail camera. "I thought I had two of these here," I said, thinking out loud. I checked over my rucksack and made sure I was ready to go. I'd pick up lunch at the diner. Maybe while I was there I'd run into my childhood friend Dave, who just happened to be the sheriff. I was out the door before the sun had risen.

Day broke, and the sun came out on my short drive, and soon I found myself once again on the back side of the Collier farm. The plan was to take a quick look at the spot Ember and I had investigated the day before, then get back to the house to take her to school, and finally to go to my next job. Taking Em to school would help me get back in Maria's good graces.

I pulled out my compass and found the direction I needed to go, using the bearing I had taken the day before. Although I had a pretty good idea where I was heading, I liked to keep in practice with my compass, and I knew I wouldn't waste time looking around after I had consulted it. When I got closer to the spot, I noticed some broken branches from where the woman had come through the day before. I noticed them because the branches were still green, not dead, and they were more or less folded over at the break. And when I looked down, I saw the leaves turned over from her footsteps.

I squatted down on my haunches to get a lower and closer look. By doing so, I could just about tell the exact path she took. Maybe it was from years of tracking or maybe it was a gift, but it was almost like the path became clear and everything else was blurred out. Standing up, I looked around to soak in my surroundings for a minute.

I loved the sounds of the forest. I smelled the pine trees, and I noticed the rays of light coming down through the canopy of the trees. I thanked the good Lord for the beauty and splendor He had created, then got back to work looking for the turned-over ground. It didn't take me long, with the bearing and my ability to track, to find the exact spot we had visited the day before. I could smell the dirt, and I estimated the size of the mound to be about two feet wide and five feet long. A sense of dread filled me when the first thing I thought of was a grave. I literally shook my head. "There's no way. This has to be a coincidence," I mumbled to myself. I looked around to appraise my situation, then found a stick that I could use for digging. I had started to plow up the loose dirt when I found a piece of red material about a foot down in the middle of the heap. I grabbed it and gave it a tug, but it still seemed to be attached to something and wouldn't come out. I started to dig some more, but then I heard a sound. I stopped immediately to listen.

It was someone talking—a woman's voice. It's her! I quickly began to rake the ground back over the hole, then, thinking quickly, pulled out my knife and cut a piece of the material off. I stuck it in my pocket and finished covering up the hole. I got to my feet and found concealment behind some heavy brush.

She came into sight, walking and talking on a phone. I thought to myself, How in the world is she getting service out here? I never have service when I need it. But as she moved closer, I could see she was talking on a satellite phone. Holy cow, who can afford a sat-phone like that? I wondered. I couldn't make out what she was saying, and I had to hunker down even more so as not to be seen.

She stopped walking and talking, and everything went quiet, except for the sound of the blood that was rushing in my ears from the adrenaline spike. I had to calm down and focus. I peeked through the shrubbery and saw her looking down at the dig site. Then she slowly raised her head and looked around. Once again, I tried to make myself smaller in hopes of not being noticed.

"I'll have to call you back," she spoke into the phone as she pulled it away from her ear and pushed a button to disconnect the call. She placed it in a pouch on the side of her belt and started to walk back in the direction she came. When she was out of sight, I slowly crept out from my hiding spot and headed back to what I was then calling "the grave." My mind was reeling with crazy ideas and questions as I contemplated the ground.

"What did you find there?" said a loud voice from behind me. I spun around to find her coming back toward me.

How did she get so close, so fast?

"Something has been digging here, probably turkeys looking for something to eat," I said without a pause.

"Oh, yeah, I bet turkey hunting is pretty good around here," she said, seemingly trying to take control of the conversation.

I fired back, "Not bad if you know what you're looking for. Take this hillside, for instance. It's full of coyote markings."

She looked at me through squinted eyes, then she slowly produced a smile. A fake smile, I was sure. "Hey, don't I know you? Oh, yeah…" She answered before I had a chance to. "You're the 'caretaker' of these woods."

"Yes, I guess I am, and by the way…what are you doing back out here?"

"I've got permission to be out here now. Oh, you didn't know?" She smirked.

I thought about it for a minute, but I felt like my prolonged silence would give her the upper hand. I needed an intelligent response—and quick. But nothing came to mind.

"Yeah, the old man said I could work my guide service through here. I'm a wilderness guide and survival instructor. My name is Niki." She offered a gloved hand.

It took me a second or two to process her words. "Nice to meet you, Niki. I'm John." I left out my last name; after all, she'd left out hers. "Funny thing, I do the same kind of work."

"Yeah, I know," she said, again catching me off guard. "I've only recently moved to the area."

There was so much I wanted to grill her on, because so much of what she was saying didn't set right with me. I started with her trade skills. "What kind of shelters are you setting up? Do your groups use tents? Because the last time I saw you, you were with a bunch of young girls who were traveling extremely light."

Without hesitation, she responded, "I teach them how to build natural shelters. Sometimes we use a lightweight tarp when the weather gets rough."

"Do you guys build fires? I've not seen any remains of fires around here or on the federal land."

"No, we mostly use small fold-up or backpacking stoves."

My first thought was that she was a liar! I had no reason to doubt her, really; it was just a feeling in my gut. Even though her responses were plausible, I still thought she was lying. She'd likely been reading survival magazines and watched videos on the internet.

Then, out of nowhere, the rain started pouring down on us like it was coming from a bucket. I looked up thinking I had been so involved with all of this I'd forgotten to keep an eye on the weather—an amateur mistake. I then glanced back at her and saw that she was doing the same thing, looking up at the sky in disbelief. Okay, maybe she wasn't lying. Maybe she was legit.

"I believe that's my cue," she said as she pulled her hood up over her blond ponytail. "Until next time, John." She did an about-face and headed off before I could come up with anything intelligent to say. Then I realized she had a rain jacket on, and I was the one standing there getting soaked —I was the one who wasn't prepared.

The rain took over everything, and I trudged back through the mud to the truck. Maybe I was the novice.

CHAPTER SEVEN

Ember

School wasn't very productive for me the next day. I had been so distracted with planning what I would be doing with what I had seen that I had barely paid any attention. I could tell that my teachers took notice, as I was usually first to raise my hand to most of their questions. Even my friends had noticed my distance as I scurried from class to class, making as little small talk as possible. There was too much on my mind, and I was afraid that if I spoke to someone, all of it would come flooding out.

During our lunch break, I shuffled to my locker and rummaged through my backpack for my field journal. It was a little book I carried that contained notes about each hike I had taken, sketches of plants and shelters, and even ideas for things I wanted to do in the future.

Slamming my locker shut, I jumped as my friend Chelsea appeared out of nowhere.

"Boo! Did I scare you?"

"Yeah, I guess you did."

I had dropped my field journal when she startled me, and Chelsea reached down to pick it up. "Hehe, sorry. I've got something to tell you that might make up for it. Mrs. Dervich said we can be writing partners for the Native American history module assignment. I know it's still a week or two away before we even need to start on it, but considering we'll be doing a presentation on it..."

"Right, a head start sounds smart."

"Exactly. What do you think? Who's our favorite Native American? I like Sacagawea."

"I don't know. I did a report on Sacagawea in second grade. Why don't we meet up sometime after school soon to start working on it? I need to go work on something in the library right now."

She shrugged at that. "Okay, that sounds fine. I'll talk to my mom about it."

As I turned to leave, Chelsea stopped me once more. "Hey, Em?"

"Yeah, Chels?"

"If something was wrong, you'd tell me, right?"

I could feel Chelsea's confusion. Did she know I was hiding something? We always told each other everything, but I didn't want her to know what I was planning until after I had thought over every aspect of the plan.

I also planned on going alone.

"Yeah, I'm just working on a personal thing right now. It's nothing to worry about, I promise."

The library was my favorite spot in the entire school. Our building wasn't new, having been built in the early sixties. Not much had changed since then, especially in the library. Tall windows usually let sunlight stream through onto the tables where you could study on your own time, but on that day, rain beat against the panes and the ambience leaked into the room like a pool of gray. With that said, the library wasn't very well lit that day, either. The idea of the structure of the library was to take advantage of natural lighting to help cut the cost of electricity, but each table still had its own lamp. Making my way to the back of the room to seclude myself, I found a desk sitting off to itself.

Alone with my tuna sandwich and a bag of carrots, I started jotting down in my field journal the thoughts that had been swirling around my head all morning:

Pack rucksack with flashlight, compass, and tarp.

Get someone to drive me to the Colliers' property.

Head back to the spot where I last saw the woman.

Take photos and gather any evidence I find. Compile them here in field journal.

Return with information—then share with Dad or wait?

Excitement and adrenaline started coursing through me, and I couldn't help but smile hard and clap quickly to myself in that strained, awkward way Dad would tease me for. I then stretched my arms and leaned back to eat my sandwich. It was then that a poster on the wall caught my attention. In big bold letters it read: GREAT GRADES LEAD TO GREAT CAREERS. Sitting there nibbling on my sandwich, the joy I had been feeling slowly fizzled. What career could I choose in the future that would meld my love for...whatever this was. Was the thrill I was feeling coming from the fact that I was investigating something? Or was the excitement due to the idea of briefly being in those woods by myself, self-reliant, no matter how short of a time?

That would be something I had to revisit later. For now, my thoughts returned back to the subject at hand. The only person I could think of whom I could trust not to tell my parents or worry about what I was up to would be Tanner. We had grown up confiding in each other; this would be no different. I just had to convince him to drive me there.

"Hey, Miss Ember."

"Oh, hey, Mr. Frank."

The school janitor, Mr. Frank, and I had recently struck up a friendship. Most of the other students ignored him, but as Mom said, I didn't know a stranger and I thought he was a pretty nice guy. Our friendship was formed mostly in passing, our quick hellos turning into "how are you?" and then finally small conversations about where he was from and his family. From what I gathered, he had no siblings, no wife or kids. He had moved here recently from New York, and that could explain what I only assumed was a Brooklyn accent.

"I can usually find you here during lunch. You're a loner, aren't you?"

I laughed at that. "Well, I do like this little alcove of mine, but I'm also kind of a social bug. You take your lunch yet?"

Mr. Frank set the trash bags down on his cart, took a quick glance around, and grabbed a candy bar from his pocket.

"I'm always ready for a snack."

Just then the bell rang.

"Always prepared, that's the way to be! Well, I gotta scoot along. Hopefully the rest of the day flies by."

"I hear that."

Instead, I found the rest of the day to drag by. The rain didn't let up; it continued to beat down on us students as school let out and we ran to our rides. Dad was waiting for me as I made my way to the parking lot.

The evening was filled with renewed energy. I couldn't wait to get back into the woods; I couldn't wait to grab my bag and go. It just wasn't time yet.

"Slow down on your food, Ember. Taste it at least!"

"Sorry, Mom," I swallowed. "It's just so good."

Mom went to ladle some more soup into my bowl.

"If I'd known you liked butternut squash soup so much, I would've made it sooner. This recipe is okay in my opinion. I think I might change it up next time, though. How was work today, Tanner?"

Tanner shrugged. "It w-wasn't too bad. I'm g-getting better at it."

Do they know? I shoot a look over to Tanner.

He gave me a knowing look, then looked away.

So not yet, then... He'll tell them after his first trap maybe.

"So...this woman I met leading a group of girls across the Colliers' land was back," Dad spoke up.

That caught my attention.

"Really?" Mom asked. "What were they doing out there? Did you see them, too, Ember?"

"No, Maria, they were hiking while I was out the other day, and today she was all alone. She says she's a field guide. I'm not sure if she's completely telling the truth, but she lets on like she knows something about survivalism. I feel like there's more than what meets the eye, though. She seems to be covering up something…but maybe I'm just reading into things."

"Maybe you're just jealous you're not the only one out in those woods anymore," Mom joked.

I thought back to the hole the woman had been filling when I last saw her. If something was being covered up, maybe I'd find out soon what it was.

"Mom, Dad, I was thinking. Could Tanner pick me up from school tomorrow? I might stay a little later to work with Chelsea on our history project. I don't know yet, though. Is that okay?"

Mom met eyes with Dad, who shrugged and nodded. "That's fine," he said. "I guess. I've got work to do, anyway. Is that okay with you, Maria?"

"Yes, and why don't you bring up the woman you found in the woods to Dave, John?"

"That's actually a good idea."

I got up to put my dishes in the sink, then moved quickly to push my chair in.

"Do you mind if I head down to my room now?"

"Yes, that's fine. Ember?"

I turned back around.

"Yes, Dad?"

The room grew quiet as Dad stared me in the eye.

"Don't you go prodding around, you hear? We don't know enough about this woman."

I slowly nodded my head as my heart quickened. I was at a crossroads. As I headed down to my room, I couldn't help but wonder...

Would curiosity kill the cat?

Thoughts swirled around my head as I sat, propped up against my bed. I slid down sideways into a lying position, face pressed against the cool floor. I felt hot, full of tension. I could feel it chewing away at me, the desire to carry out my plan. The desire for knowledge.

What did she bury?

What did Dad see?

Did he look in the right place?

He was just trying to protect me...but I was a capable woman. I wasn't his little girl anymore. I was sixteen years old! I was stronger than that. I could prove it. I needed to show him!

"Am I still gonna pick you up?" Tanner pulled me out of my thoughts.

"What?"

"You can't fool me, Em. I know what you're going to do. N-no one can keep you away from what you want."

"Yeah...I guess. I need to go check my pack if I'm going to follow through with this."

I crept up the stairs and back into the kitchen. Opening the door slowly, I listened for signs of Mom and Dad and heard the sound of Mom washing the dishes. I knew that her back would be toward the door of the basement, so I crept into the kitchen, then snuck over to the door that led out to the back porch.

Running out into the cool night air, I passed quickly through the yard toward the garage. Trying to stay out of the direct view of any of the windows, I caught a glimpse of Dad at work in the garage. It was time to act casual.

"Hey, Dad, what are you up to?"

Dad put down his tools and picked up a piece of leather.

"Hey, kiddo, just working on a knife sheath for trading. I need a new belt for my sander."

I took the piece of leather in my hands and turned it to find a coiled snake imprinted on the leather.

"Wow...a rattlesnake?"

Dad smiled.

"Copperhead."

The air inside the garage was calming, a familiar feeling I'd known since childhood. The dusty shelves were lined with tools, the scent of sawdust was in the air, and a quiet peace filled the area as Dad worked on the project at hand.

He had only a single lamp above him as he worked. A few lanterns were lit around the room, giving off a warm glow. I walked over to my shelf and looked into my bag. Everything was there, alright, just as I had left it. I specifically wanted my folding shovel and knife saw. I looked up and saw hanging above me on the wall the atlatl Dad had made when I was ten years old. The carved tool was still as I remembered it: smooth and simple, as ready to be used as it was the day he finished it. That was around the time I started really taking an interest in what Dad did, what we did now.

"It's important to learn how to turn what is around you to your benefit in a survival scenario. That, and never let people know just how prepared you are in any

situation—*you always want the element of surprise."*

His words had stayed with me since that day, and I could feel my father's eyes on my back, watching me even now.

CHAPTER EIGHT

John

A few days after the second encounter with Niki, I decided to get some advice and maybe even some help. I had made plans to meet my closest and most trusted friends at the local diner for breakfast. That morning I woke up and hit the ground running with determination.

I liked to think of us men, and sometimes our families, as a pack. The guys hung out all the time, and often we included our families. We didn't always run together, but when we needed each other the most, we were there for each other.

My friend Jeff was a funny person, with a very dry sense of humor. Skinny and wiry, he was always up for an adventure. He worked for a delivery company, and time was always of the essence for him. Did I mention he didn't have a filter? By that, I mean he always said the first thing that came to his mind, no matter what. He was a great guy, though, and he meant well, but he could dish out tough love—even when you didn't ask for it.

Robert was the third of the three amigos, and he was different but the same. He was tall and stocky, built like a tank, but he was also timid and sweet. He was very reliable, he loved everyone, and he always looked for the best in people—even to a fault. He owned the local flower shop and he knew everyone—and I mean everyone.

I walked into the diner on time, but my two compadres were already seated, laughing and joking as usual. When we got together, it was always a lot of laughs, even at funerals, but that was likely Jeff's fault. I grabbed a chair and could already feel myself smiling before I was seated. The laughter was contagious. Soon we were eating and chuckling, reminiscing about old memories and creating new ones as we went along.

Jeff finally switched the gears with a question. "So, what's all this about? I mean the meeting you called here."

For a little while I had forgotten about Niki and all of my life's problems. Back to reality, "Well, I've got a strange set of circumstances to discuss with you guys." Robert looked down at my plate as I began. "Em and I have stumbled across something very strange in the woods. We were out at Old Man Collier's farm when it happened."

Robert took a piece of toast and started to clean the remains of breakfast from his plate. He shoved it in his mouth, chewed twice, then swallowed. "What do you mean 'strange'?"

"Yeah, that's pretty vague, considering how strange I am," Jeff added.

I looked at them both as they stared back at me waiting for my response. "You guys are going to think I'm crazy, but here goes." I recounted the events that had occurred over the last few days as they each listened intently—except for Robert's occasional glance down at what was left on my plate. After going to great pains to share every last detail, I finished with, "So, tell me how crazy I am."

I realized they both were on the edge of their seats, literally leaning forward. They simultaneously sat back and shot each other a long glance. Then they looked at me.

"Holy cow," Robert finally drew out slowly.

"Holy cow is right," Jeff seconded. "I think you have uncovered something big. Huge!"

"So, you don't think I'm crazy, imagining things?"

"No way, but the only way to be sure is to investigate," Robert said with a grin. Robert was the kind of person who would rather listen to the police scanner than the radio, and given the chance, he'd chase a fire truck to see where it was going. "Here's what I've got in mind."

I interrupted. "Wait a minute, let's not get carried away here. I haven't even spoken to Dave about this yet. I just wanted to be sure I wasn't insane."

Jeff turned in his chair. "No, you're right. Let's not get crazy here. We need to look into this ourselves before you tell the sheriff."

"Wait, wait, wait!" I said. "We can't go invading someone's privacy, just because she gives me bad vibes." All was quiet as we took turns looking at each other.

Rob finally spoke. "You going to finish those eggs?" He pointed to my plate. I pushed it over to him without hesitation. I knew better than to get between a predator and his prey.

"Look, if we do this, we've got to be discreet," I said, conceding.

"John," Jeff said with a smirk. "We both have the perfect cover. I'm a delivery guy, Robert owns a flower shop, and sometimes he does the deliveries when things are busy. What better camouflage is there than that?"

"Are you guys familiar with surveillance techniques?" I asked.

"Cool! I've always wanted to do some private investigating," Robert said.

"I've watched some videos on it," Jeff added.

I launched into an abbreviated version of how to conduct surveillance. "You've got the cover, now let's talk about the technique. It's about how to hide in plain sight."

Robert looked down at himself and his bulk, then looked at me with raised eyebrows.

"Yes, Robert, even you can do this. Our main objective here is to find out as much about her and get as much intelligent information as possible without breaking any laws. There is a thing called the Plain View Doctrine, which allows us to observe people from public access points without getting into trouble. If we can find something that could be considered probable cause for the authorities to investigate, that would be great.

"But before we do our surveillance, we need to do some reconnaissance. We need to find out where exactly she lives. I already know what she drives because I've seen it. It's a black late-model SUV. I'm pretty sure she carries a weapon"—I saw her reach for it behind her back—"but there is no solid proof on that. Once we establish these things, then we can figure out if she has any other associates and her routines.

"Jeff, keep your delivery hat on at all times, and Robert, wear a hat. Pick a shady spot, preferably between two other cars if possible. Stay in your vehicles and watch from a distance—and please, do not get caught."

Jeff looked at me with bright eyes. "I know, we're disavowed if we get caught, just like in the movies."

"Yeah, and I don't want to have to explain to Dave why he's arresting you and I'm bailing you out," I responded. "We'll be using our cell phones and three-way calling to communicate. Don't forget to use the earbuds that came with your phone—they have a built-in microphone so you won't have to draw attention to yourself when talking."

Robert rubbed his jaw as he looked at the ceiling. "I'm not sure where mine are at. I might have to buy some new ones."

"Whatever," I replied. "As long as they work and help conceal the fact that you are talking on the phone. After we gather enough information, we'll decide what to do with it, and I'll take it to Dave if necessary."

We all sat quietly for the next few minutes, finishing what was left of breakfast and contemplating the job before us. Eventually the silence was broken when the waitress brought over the check. We parted ways after we had paid for our breakfast, and we began our assigned tasks.

CHAPTER NINE

Ember

My thoughts traveled back to when Dad and I were in the woods the other day. Scenes of that afternoon played out in my head and spilled onto my sketchbook.

The hole the woman was trying to fill with dirt—what was in it?

Remembering my gut-wrenching nerves and the leaves scattering as I fell forward in fear of being shot, I smirked. It wasn't even the woman who was doing the shooting and I had freaked out so bad.

"Is something funny, Miss Derick?"

The reality of where I was came back to me as my eyes darted toward my teacher.

"No, sir, I'm sorry."

"Let's pay attention to the class, then."

As Mr. Wilson turned back around to continue the algebraic equation, my body remained present, but my mind wasn't.

Chelsea met up with me after class, and we headed to study hall in the library. I wanted to gather her thoughts on the matter. We headed toward the back of the library, to my favorite spot, and we dropped our bags beside the table before sitting down.

"So, Chels," I whispered, "I've got something I want to talk to you about, but you've got to promise to keep it a secret."

Chelsea leaned in and looked me straight in the eye as she smirked. "I've got something better than what you're probably going to tell me."

"I doubt that!"

"I found out that cute guy you noticed in church is named Isaac, and he's in my biology class! Homecoming is this weekend —maybe you could ask him to the dance… Or I could drop a hint for him to ask you!"

Oh, I hadn't even realized. Even though it was tempting to hang out with the new cute boy now known as Isaac, apparently Chelsea had forgotten that dances and parties were not my thing.

"That's great and all, but you know I'd rather be out sketching in the woods than going to a dance. Anyway, I've got to tell you about something I actually saw in the woods."

I leaned in closer and whispered the events of the other day in her ear. Her blue eyes widened as I told her, and her dark curly hair bounced as she turned her head to see if anyone was watching us.

"Em! That's crazy, you could've been shot!"

"No, that's not what I'm so worried about. What do you think about what I saw—that hole being filled in?"

Chelsea sat back, brow furrowed and eyes scanning the wall directly behind me.

"Honestly, Em, it could be anything at this point. I've heard my dad telling my mom about your dad's concerns. Nothing sounds serious, though."

I shrugged. "I just don't know... I have this hunch..."

Having looked up, we met eyes and all at once Chelsea understood.

"Something isn't right, something in those woods is calling me to look deeper into this."

More students were coming into the library, and the sounds of shuffled feet and tossed bags onto desks filled the room. The shushing of the librarian rose above the clamor.

"I mean it, Chels, I need to go look."

Chelsea shook her head, her curls bouncing back and forth. Her hands moved to the back of her neck, as a look of concern came over her face.

"Ember, it's crazy. If something is really going on, which I doubt it is, you shouldn't be going after it. Especially not alone. I don't like this. I don't like those woods."

She never had. As long as I'd known her, she'd been afraid of the forest in general. She said there was something to be said for "modern civilization." I didn't share those views.

I closed my eyes, and suddenly I was with Dad, bouncing along in the truck, traveling down the road that passed through the forest. The sun shone through the leaves, and I rested on the door's window frame, chin on my arm. With the window rolled down, my hand reached out into the summer air and felt the rush of it through my fingers. No pending responsibilities gripped me, no wanting, just the grateful feeling that was planted deep in my heart—a warm feeling of thankfulness that went from my messy hair, to my T-shirt and ratty jeans, right down to my worn boots, for the rocky soil my feet hit as I slid out of the truck after we stopped. Dad grabbed the poles from the back of the truck, and I grabbed the tackle. We headed through the edge of the forest and down a single-track path to a little clearing where the lake rested. Few words were spoken there; only the birds called out into the silence. The sun dappled across the rippling water, and reflections of the cool water pooled in my eyes. On those sandy-soiled shores I would lie on my back as I watched my pole propped up in the rocks and the line gently bobbing up and down. A breeze gently pulled wisps of my hair across my face. I considered pulling it back behind my ears, but instead let it continuously carelessly wave as I watched a pair of dragonflies dance in courtship, lazily carried off by that same breeze.

No, the forest was sacred to me. It was the place I went when I needed to find a connection to nature, a place to go and talk with God. Those hidden treasures of the forest, bright with pleasant memories, were now being overtaken with menacing storm clouds of doubt and fear in the back of my mind. I had to get answers. I needed to understand what was going on there so that the forest could return to being the safe haven it should be for everyone.

All of my doubts and concern could have simply been the result of my imagination, but I had to have proof either way. Those dark clouds had to be called away, the oncoming storm quelled.

Now, as I watched Chelsea pulling out her study material, I knew she didn't feel the same. So, with that, I stared blankly at my textbook, but the words meshed together in a blur as my thoughts remained on what I'd rather be doing. I had to stop all of it. My grades would suffer if I didn't get my act together.

Once the bell rang, I ran out to meet Tanner. It was his day to pick me up from school, and he had previously agreed to take me out to the part of the forest where the conspicuous hole lay, waiting to be investigated.

CHAPTER TEN

We barely spoke as Tanner drove us down the same road that I had traveled with Dad those many summers ago. Instead of rays of sun streaking across the sky, today was a gray day, with no hint of the sun's glow in sight. Drops of rain started gently pelting the windows, and I watched the trees pass by my window in some sort of watchful, solemn way. It was like the forest was becoming a stranger to me.

Perhaps I was learning an important lesson: Nothing is ever as it seems. Nothing is ever as it was.

We turned down a rural road and parked near where the Collier's land and the forest met.

"I won't be long. I think it's about a twenty-minute hike that way," I said.

The rain didn't let up, but it wasn't getting worse. Tanner stared ahead and watched the windshield wipers swish back and forth. He looked doubtful about what was taking place.

"If you're not back in an hour, I'm coming in after you."

"Sure."

I slung my pack over my shoulders, shut the door, and started climbing my way up the steep hillside. My hands grabbed trees for support, and dirt pressed against my pants as my boots dug deep into the soil. My ascent would be one of many as I hiked my way through the lazy drizzle. It was quiet; all I could hear was the rain hitting the canopy of leaves above. The sound was comforting, almost like the sound it made on the shelters Dad would make out of tarps when we were camping outside.

I checked my compass, making sure I was still going the right way. Continuing through the forest, I pushed through brush and mud until I came to the place where I had found myself a few days ago. I could still see the place where my cover had been blown as I slid down the embankment. So much for stealth.

After having descended the hillside, I finally stood on that freshly placed soil. I had to be careful not to leave behind too many traces of my presence. After checking my watch, I noticed that I had only half an hour left. A thought came to me, and I took off my pack to search for my cell phone.

Snap—flash.

The noise of the artificial shutter broke the natural sounds of the forest. I took a photo of the ground—and how someone had attempted to hide the spot with the placement of cut brush.

Snap—flash.

Another photo of my surroundings for reference.

I kicked the brush aside, clearing away the debris so I could further my inspection.

Dropping to my knees, I pulled out my e-tool from my pack. Rearing back, and then letting out a breath to steady my nerves, I stabbed into the muddy soil and thrusted it to the side. Not sure what to even look for, I simply continued to move the earth over and over and over again. I grew filthy and exasperated.

Nothing.

Something had to be here, though— why else would someone dig a hole and then fill it back in?

Well, I hadn't seen her dig the hole, but I had seen her piling dirt into it. Looking at my watch, I noticed that there were ten minutes left before the hour deadline my brother had given me was up.

Countless more minutes went by, and the rain started to let up. Letting out a groan, I debated on piling what measly amount of dirt I had moved back into the hole. There it was, though, in the back of my mind: that faint feeling that was growing into a flame of persistence. The rain stopped altogether, and with that my hope grew even more. I started digging faster, soon tossing the e-tool to the side and clawing my way through the dirt, feeling for anything.

Then I spotted it.

Standing out from the brown and green of the forest was a bit of red, a frayed piece of fabric. Looking closer, I realized that it was part of the red flowered scarf the sickly-looking girl had been wearing, the girl whom Dad had told me about.

Did it mean there was more to be uncovered in that spot, deep in the solitude of the forest? Dad was going to flip out. I needed photographic evidence! I grabbed my phone once more.

Snap—flash.

I took a photo of the spot once more. Then, grabbing the fabric between my fingers, I slowly started pulling it up from the dirt. As it rose, the soft earth began to give way to reveal that something larger lay beneath the soil: the wrist of an arm to which the fabric had been tied.

I froze. The world stood still for a moment before the sky suddenly opened with a heavy, drenching downpour. There was a terrible crash of thunder moments after lightning flashed, frightening me. I jumped up, scrabbling backward on my hands and feet, and I dropped the piece of fabric. The hand attached to the wrist I had uncovered fell onto the overturned soil. My body was racked with nerves as a chill ran down my spine. I began to shiver, and whether it was from the soaking rain and my clothes sticking to me or the horrific shock I was now in, I did not know. Paranoid, my eyes darted around, scanning the forest to be sure that I was alone.

Now, I'm not sure that a person is ever truly alone. But at that moment, I felt like I was being watched. Not realizing that I had crawled my way up against a large tree and curled into a fetal position, I found myself wanting to shrink into a hole and hide. I should've listened to Chelsea. I shouldn't have come back.

But then all the years of Dad's training, all of the self-reliance and the confidence he had instilled in me came flooding back, and I realized that I would be in a bad position if I stayed. The storm was so loud, I couldn't possibly hear anything or anyone approaching. And due to the awful downpour, I could barely see the distance back to what I then knew was a shallow grave.

Time was running out, and the storm was getting worse. I could smell the electricity of the lightning in the air, and the hair on my arms was standing up. My ears were ringing after each crash of thunder. The storm had to have been right on top of me. With my thoughts starting to come together, I shakily gathered my nerve and moved onto my hands and knees. I placed my hand against the tree. Slowly rising to my feet and planting them firmly on the ground, I stood against the tempest.

It wasn't about me anymore. No, the fear was gone, and I became fiercely determined. It was about the poor girl whose body had been dumped like some meaningless trash. As I rushed back to the gravesite, I was filled with a sense of sadness. Who would bring her justice? She was all alone out there; no one knew where she was.

I knelt onto the puddling ground and started scooping up the mud in my hands. Not wanting to add to the desecration of her resting place, and with as much respect as I could, I quickly smoothed the dirt back over the girl's remains. Placing the brush back onto the grave, I called out over the chaos of the storm.

"I will be back for you!"

After shoving my gear back into my pack, I started sprinting through the forest back to my waiting brother. Tanner and I had to get this back to Dad and into the right hands.

My pack, slung over my shoulder, bounced against my body as I flew through the forest. Mud slapped against my boots and pants, and the rain still came down hard, I tried to get back as quickly as possible. A root caught my foot, tripping me. I landed right on my face, entirely filthy. Picking myself up, I pulled both of my arms through the straps of my bag and picked up the pace once more. When my adrenaline started waning, my legs started growing heavy and my arms grew weak. My heart was still racing, though, at the urgency of getting back.

I ran to the point where the forest met the road, and with a leap of faith, I jumped over the last bit of brush and landed with a jolt at the top of the slope of the hillside. Due to the loose rock, or the scree, I began to glissade down the unstable terrain. Dad taught me that glissading was a speedy way to slide down a steep hillside. It was like sledding on my butt, but without the sled. Sitting down, I lowered my center of gravity to lessen my chances of falling.

I slid my way into view of Tanner, his impatient figure resting against the car.

"Y-you're about thirty minutes late."

"I know, but we've got to go now!"

Rushing around the side of the car, I flung the passenger-side door open, tossed my bag onto the floorboard, and hopped in.

"R-really? You're filthy, Em! W-what's wrong?"

Taking note of my urgency, he started the car and peeled out onto the road. My heart still pounded, and I was trying to catch my breath.

"W-what is it, Ember? What's wrong?"

"I found something serious."

His eyes darted sideways to see me digging through my pack. I pulled out my cell phone.

"I knew you shouldn't have gone out there."

"You wouldn't believe what I found, though, Tanner... We need to get these photos to Dad now!"

Grabbing my phone from my bag, I wiped the grime off of it and pulled up the picture I had taken of the fabric tied to a human wrist. Tanner's eyes darted from the road to the photo.

"What in the world did you find, Em? What have you done?"

"It's not what I've done, it's what someone else has done! I'm calling Dad."

I hit the speed-dial, but it felt like the phone rang forever before Dad picked up.

"Hey, kiddo, what's up?"

It all started pouring out of me as I placed the phone on speaker and spoke quickly.

"Dad! I went into the forest and back to that spot! I found something—I found someone!"

"Wait, what? Ember, slow down. You're not making sense."

Tanner leaned in to speak over me.

"Dad, Em found a—"

Suddenly the car slid out of control, and the sound of shattering glass and the screeching of the crunching of metal filled my ears.

A sharp pain filled my head before the darkness enveloped me.